BROWNIES AND DARK SHADOWS

A SANDY BAY COZY MYSTERY

AMBER CREWES

PEN-N-A-PAD PUBLISHING

Copyright © Pen-n-a-Pad Publishing

First published in July 2018

All characters and events in this publication, other than those clearly in the public domain, are fictitious and any resemblance to real persons, living or dead, is purely coincidental.

Copyright © Pen-n-a-Pad Publishing

The moral right of the author has been asserted.

All rights reserved. This book or any portion thereof may not be reproduced or used in any manner whatsoever without the express written permission of the publisher except for the use of brief quotations in a book review.

For questions and comments about this book, please contact info@ambercrewes.com

ISBN: 9781718015203
Imprint: Independently Published

OTHER BOOKS IN THE SANDY BAY
SERIES

Apple Pie and Trouble
Brownies and Dark Shadows
Cookies and Buried Secrets
Donuts and Disaster
Éclairs and Lethal Layers

A SANDY BAY COZY MYSTERY

BOOK TWO

1

"I cannot *believe* we booked the Weeks Group corporate order!" Lori squealed, her eyes dancing with excitement.

Meghan smiled warmly at Lori. It had been a pleasant surprise to book such a lucrative deal; the Weeks Group was one of the largest companies on the West Coast, and Meghan knew what an honor it was for her bakery, Truly Sweet, to be chosen as the official bakery of the company. The bakery hadn't even been open for a year yet, and already, Meghan's business was the talk of the town!

"Just think, Meghan! Every restaurant and cafe at the Weeks Group will be filled with *your* sweets!" Lori exclaimed.

Meghan smiled down at Lori, her new assistant. Lori had only been working as Meghan's assistant for a few weeks, but Meghan adored Lori's warmth and enthusiasm. As the two women tied their aprons in the bakery's backroom and prepared for the day ahead, Meghan's heart swelled with gratitude for her protégé.

"*Our* sweets, Lori," Meghan gently corrected, placing a hand softly on Lori's shoulder. "You are my assistant now, Lori! You are a member of the team here. My success is *our* success, and I want you to know how proud I am of how quickly you've learned about the way I do things here at Truly Sweet!"

Lori beamed, her youthful face glowing with Meghan's kind words. At twenty-two, she was only a few years younger than Meghan, but her earnest spirit made her seem even younger than her age. Meghan enjoyed Lori's company, and she was thankful to have a new friend in her adopted hometown; Meghan had only recently moved to Sandy Bay, and with every kindred spirit found, she felt even more at home.

Meghan tucked a loose strand of dark hair behind her ear and finished tying her apron. She walked to the large sink in the backroom and washed her hands, careful to scrub every inch.

"Do we have a busy day today, Meghan?" Lori asked, wiping her own damp hands on her apron as she walked into the front room. Meghan shook her head.

"No," Meghan replied. "I received the call about the Weeks Group corporate order last night, and I went ahead and cleared our schedule for the week so that we can begin preparing! It will be an ongoing order, and I expect it will keep us busy. We'll have a few miscellaneous orders to fill this week, and surely some walk-in customers, but otherwise, it will be a quiet week!"

Meghan had barely finished her sentence before the bakery was abuzz with activity; suddenly, the tiny silver bells attached to the front door chimed as the door burst open. A petite, blonde-haired woman marched up to the front counter, the two strands of milky-white pearls around her neck jingling as she moved.

"Meghan Truman! You are *just* the person I need to speak with!"

Meghan's eyes widened as Kirsty Fisher sauntered up to the counter. Her heart sank; Kirsty was one of Sandy Bay's more influential residents, and she had acted aloof toward Meghan since the scandal that had threatened Truly Sweet's success only weeks ago. Kirsty had hardly acknowledged Meghan since the murder of Norman Butcher, a local man, had been blamed on Meghan and her treats. Even though Meghan's name had been cleared for weeks now, Kirsty's attitude had still been chilly. Meghan felt her hands quiver as Kirsty approached, and she bit her bottom lip nervously as Kirsty's lips turned upward into a business-like smile.

"Lori," Meghan hissed under her breath, trying to capture the attention of her trusted assistant who was rolling out dough behind her. Lori heard Meghan's whisper and immediately came to her side.

"Well, good morning, Kirsty!" Lori said kindly to the woman as she wiped her messy hands on her apron. "What brings you in this morning?"

Meghan's shoulders dropped in relief; a lifetime resident of Sandy Bay, Lori knew how to interact with *everyone* in town, and Meghan was thankful for her help as Kirsty eyed her.

Kirsty nodded at Lori, but quickly moved her attention back to Meghan.

"Meghan, dear! So lovely to see you. I hope you are well?"

Meghan shrugged nervously, and Kirsty continued.

"So Meghan, I've heard you bake the *best* brownies in town! Your bakery was the talk of the town over the last few weeks, you know, with… everything… that happened?"

Meghan watched as Lori disappeared into the backroom. The scandal had involved Lori; it was her father that had been murdered, and while he and Lori had not had a close relationship, Meghan knew Lori was still recovering from the loss.

"Anyway, I'm *so* terribly sorry that your first few weeks in Sandy Bay were tainted with such a scandal! How awful. This is such a lovely town, and I don't want you to get the wrong idea of us!" Kirsty said, her smile shifting into a look of concern.

Meghan shook her head. "It's alright," she replied. "My bakery's reputation has been restored, and I think things have settled down."

Kirsty gave Meghan a pitying smile.

"Well, I heard that your name was cleared. That's so wonderful. I just had a little idea that could help completely eliminate *any* more issues you may have been having because of that horrible little scandal!" Kirsty said, tossing her blonde hair behind her shoulders and retrieving a business card from her purse. "As you know, I run the Fisher Foundation, the biggest charity in town. We raise money for those in need, and it's nearly time for our annual gala, the Fisher Fest! My caterer unexpectedly canceled, and the new caterer will not be providing desserts. Since you are in need of some positive exposure in town, especially given that tricky little incident with Mr. Butcher, I thought it might be nice if you could provide some desserts for the gala!"

Meghan stared at Kirsty, her hazel eyes growing large. She took a long, silent breath, considering Kirsty's proposal.

"Well?" Kirsty asked, beginning to tap her high heels impatiently on the wooden floor.

"I don't know," Meghan finally answered. "I just took on a major corporate order, and I don't know if I have the time to make even more brownies with the commitment I just made."

Kirsty pursed her lips in a pout and batted her eyelashes at Meghan.

"Come on," Kirsty coaxed, sliding her business card across the counter. "Think about your business! This would quiet all the people still whispering about Truly Sweet, and you would have so many of Sandy Bay's finest folks sampling *your* treats at the gala!"

Meghan placed her hands on her round hips as she mentally calculated the hours she would need to bake enough desserts to take to the gala. She knew that with Lori's help, she could do it, but for some reason, she felt uneasy about accepting Kirsty's proposal.

"Meghan?" Kirsty said sternly. "I need to know if you will help us! It's for *charity*. You simply cannot turn down the opportunity to bake for a *charity*!"

"Okay," Meghan answered, folding her hands in front on her. "I'll do it."

"Excellent!" Kirsty said gleefully, snapping her purse closed and stepping back from the counter. "Here's my card. Give me a call this evening and we'll work out the details. I think you might even thank me later, Meghan! Toodles!"

As Kirsty marched out of the bakery, her tall, thin high heels clacking across the floor, Meghan leaned back against the counter.

"What did she want?" Lori asked as she walked back into the front room. "Kirsty Fisher *always* wants something; she and her husband run every event and charity in town, and no one can say no to Kirsty Fisher."

Meghan shrugged. "We're baking for the Fisher Fest," she said to Lori. Lori's eyes sparkled as she heard the news.

"The Fisher Fest!" Lori exclaimed. "That's the fanciest event all year! Kirsty even makes the caterers and workers dress up! We'll have so much fun, Meghan! This is good news!"

Meghan looked down at her shoes, her chest feeling tight.

"Meghan? This is good news! Between the Weeks Group

deal and the Fisher Fest, things are looking up for Truly Sweet!"

Meghan shook her head. "I don't know what's wrong with me," Meghan whispered. "I just have a bad feeling about this event. For some reason, Fisher Fest has me worried, Lori."

2

"These are the *best* brownies I have *ever* eaten," said an older gentleman to Meghan, as the woman with him nodded in agreement.

Meghan smiled demurely. It had been a wonderful night; guests had flocked to the little booth Meghan and Lori had hastily constructed for the event, and the girls' hard work was paying off!

"What is your name? My wife and I would *love* to have you bake for our next event," the man said kindly.

Meghan grinned. She was thankful that she had ignored her gut instinct and agreed to provide treats for the event. Kirsty Fisher was *right*; the exposure Meghan and her business were gaining was invaluable, and Meghan had given out nearly every single business card she had brought with her to the event!

"I'm Meghan Truman," she said.

"Meghan," the man repeated. "It's been a pleasure! I'm Brian Bishop, and this is my wife, Amy."

"It's a pleasure," Amy said, smiling sweetly at Meghan.

"We need to go find our sons now, but mark my words,

you will be hearing from us soon!" Brian exclaimed as he led his wife away.

Meghan smoothed her long, black velvet dress, feeling every bit the successful, revered business woman she now was. She knew she looked lovely; her dark hair was piled atop her head in an elegant chignon, and the long black gloves on her arms made her look sophisticated. Had she not been standing behind the Truly Sweet booth, Meghan could have easily been mistaken for one of the guests at Fisher Fest!

"Well, look at you, Princess!"

Meghan heard the familiar voice of Karen Denton, her former neighbor. She turned to find Karen beaming up at her.

"Karen!" she exclaimed. "I didn't know you would be here!"

Karen smiled at Meghan, looking beautiful in a pale yellow gown that made her tiny waist look even smaller. At seventy-two years old, Karen, a retired nurse, was the fittest person Meghan knew, and as Karen's eyes danced with happiness, she looked not a day older than Meghan!

"Surprise! I heard that Kirsty Fisher wrangled *you* into this little shin-dig, and I knew I couldn't miss it for the world!"

Meghan stepped out from behind the booth and embraced Karen. The two had first met several years ago back in Los Angeles. Meghan, pursuing a career in acting, had moved into a small apartment next to Karen's, and once the two had met, they were practically inseparable. Now, as they hugged amidst the glamorous guests of Fisher Fest, Meghan was grateful that Karen had first suggested Meghan explore Sandy Bay, Karen's hometown.

"It's going so well!" she whispered to Karen.

"I can see that! Everyone is talking about the brownies! I am so excited for you!"

Meghan grinned. "I wasn't so sure about saying yes, but I'm glad I did.

A mischievous look flashed across Karen's face, and she playfully bumped Meghan's hip with her own. "I heard a certain fellow stopped by to say hello to you!" she said.

Meghan's face turned red. In the first hour of the event, just as Meghan's nerves were settling down, Jack Irvin had stopped by the booth. Meghan had been bent down below the table with a brownie stuffed into her mouth when Jack approached; she had not noticed him coming, and as she kneeled down to gobble the brownie, she saw a pair of shining black dress shoes stop and stay beside her booth.

"Great work tonight."

She swallowed the brownie quickly and stood up to find Jack smiling at her. Her face burned. She had not initially warmed to Jack, but after he had helped her walk home with a sprained ankle a few weeks ago, she had been harboring a little crush on the handsome police officer.

"Thanks," Meghan said. "It's good to see you, Jack!"

He grinned, but took a hand to his mouth, exaggerating a brushing motion. Meghan was puzzled, and she could feel her chest pounding as Jack smiled at her.

"You look so nice!" Meghan said, looking at Jack's suit. "You clean up nicely!"

Jack's eyes moved from Meghan's and traveled up and down.

"You look beautiful, Meghan," he replied. Meghan felt her chest swell with excitement as Jack leaned in close over the table.

"Meghan?" he whispered. Meghan closed her eyes in anticipation; was Jack going to *kiss* her?

"Yes?" Meghan said, her hazel eyes still closed. She felt a gentle brush of Jack's hand on her face, and she flew open her eyes in shock.

"You had something on your face," he said softly. "It looked like brownie crumbs!"

Meghan was embarrassed, and Lori came to the rescue.

"Jack!" Lori said pleasantly. "Need to steal Meghan away; we're too busy for you two to be chatting!"

Lori quickly whisked Meghan away.

"That's the last time I ever eat a dessert!" she said to Lori. Lori smiled graciously, both women knowing this declaration to be untrue.

Now, as Meghan stood with Karen at the end of the event, she felt herself relax. Besides embarrassing herself in front of Jack, she had enjoyed the event and even networked! It had been a good evening, and Meghan felt the slightest bit of embarrassment at her initial indignation toward Kirsty.

"Ladies and gentlemen! Yoo-hooo!"

As if she had conjured her by thinking about her, Meghan saw Kirsty take the stage in the center of the room. Kirsty was dressed in a floor-length purple ball gown, and a handsome man stood next to her, his arm wrapped around Kirsty's small waist.

"Who is that man?" Meghan whispered to Karen.

"That's Vince, Kirsty's husband," she replied. "They are fabulously wealthy and fabulously charitable; the Fisher Foundation built a new center downtown for disadvantaged youth a few years ago, and the proceeds from tonight will go toward a scholarship fund!"

Meghan watched as Kirsty appraised the room. Several hundred guests floated about the ballroom, and Kirsty smiled as all chatter hushed.

"Thank you. My husband and I would like to thank you all for your generosity tonight! The Fisher Foundation is an integral part of Sandy Bay, and it is your generosity that helps us help others! Please give yourself a round of applause!"

The guests clapped politely, and Kirsty passed the microphone to her husband.

"Hello, all! I'm Vince Fisher, and I would like to thank you for being here!"

Meghan leaned over to Karen as the crowd again clapped for the Fishers. "They are such an attractive couple," she said, her voice tinged with longing. She watched as Kirsty gazed up at her husband, her eyes brimming with adoration. Vince returned the loving look, and Meghan turned away, feeling embarrassed at the feelings that flooded her as the Fishers exchanged such intimate looks amidst the hundreds of guests.

Karen placed an arm around Meghan's shoulder. "They are a perfect couple. We're lucky to have such a couple in Sandy Bay! But don't you worry, Meghan. You'll find someone someday who looks at you the way Kirsty and Vince look at each other. It will happen."

The Fishers thanked each vendor for their participation, and Meghan received a standing ovation for her desserts. She gave a little curtsy as the crowd cheered for her, and she knew she had made the right decision in helping Kirsty. As she and Lori tore down their booth at the end of the night, Meghan's heart was filled with joy. Her business had received significant attention at the event, Jack had seen her in her beautiful dress, and she had garnered the approval of the Fishers, one of the wealthiest, most powerful couples in town! As Meghan packed away the remaining desserts, she felt as though the best days in her new home in Sandy Bay were surely ahead of her.

3

"Thank you for coming to the rescue tonight," Kirsty cooed to Meghan as the last of the guests shuffled out of the ballroom. "Your treats were a *hit*! I didn't try them myself as I'm on a no-sugar, no-carb, no-nonsense diet, but *everyone* else was raving about them! I will certainly book you for our next event. Toodles!"

Kirsty walked away, and Meghan smiled, pleased that Truly Sweet's reputation would *finally* be free of the blemish from the murder scandal. Accepting Kirsty's proposal had been a wise business decision, and in celebration, Meghan surreptitiously pulled a brownie out of her small, beaded clutch. Feigning a cough, she moved the gloved-hand holding the brownie to her lips, eager to taste the delectable dessert that had received such wonderful attention at the Fisher Fest. Meghan stuffed the brownie into her mouth, and before she could help herself, she let out a moan of delight.

"Meghan?"

Kirsty had returned! Meghan clasped her hand to her mouth, embarrassed to have been caught in the act of eating her own brownies *again*.

"Mmhhummm," she mumbled, trying to force the brownie down her throat as Kirsty stared up at her. Her heart pounded in her chest; Kirsty was an intimidating woman, and she made Meghan nervous.

"Are you alright?" Kirsty asked, raising one eyebrow.

Meghan nodded, and *finally*, she swallowed the brownie. She used her hand to brush the crumbs off of her face and smiled at Kirsty.

"Did you need something?" she asked, her heart thundering furiously in her chest as Kirsty shook her head.

"I thought I had left my purse here, but I see that my husband has it," Kirsty said, pointing across the room at Vince. "Oh, Meghan! Thanks once more for the brownies. I wish I could have indulged! You are just so lucky; it must be *so* nice not to not even worry about your figure. Anyway, Vince and I are leaving! Thanks again! Toodles!"

Kirsty blew a kiss as she walked away, and Meghan turned back to her booth.

"What a night," Meghan murmured.

* * *

THE NEXT MORNING, Meghan let herself sleep in; she hadn't even arrived home until one in the morning, and as the late morning sunshine brightened her room, she snuggled further beneath the covers, enjoying the lazy start to the day. She had even given Lori a paid day off; Lori had been such an asset during Fisher Fest, and Meghan was pleased to return the favor.

Meghan rolled over beneath her thick, purple comforter and yawned. Her thighs ached from tottering around in high heels all night, and with only a few orders to attend to later in the afternoon, she did not see *any* reason to leave her comfortable bed until at least noon.

"Meghan! Meghan!"

Meghan propped herself up on her elbow and furrowed her brow. She wasn't expecting anyone; had she just imagined someone calling her name?

"MEGHAN!!!"

Meghan sat up in bed, pulling the comforter up to her chin. Who was yelling for her? It was a Saturday morning, and Meghan's head was foggy with exhaustion. She slowly tucked her messy dark hair into a low bun, still listening for her name and hoping that she had perhaps dreamed the sound of the shouting.

"MEGHAN! It's Lori! Meghan, you have to let me in *now!*"

"Lori?" Meghan muttered to herself as she crawled out of her bed and hastily tied on her shabby blue bathrobe. "Why on Earth is Lori here today? Did she forget I gave her the day off?"

Meghan slipped her feet into her favorite pair of brown slippers and walked downstairs. She could hear Lori shouting her name, and she tore open the door to find her assistant in tears.

"Lori?" she asked, her voice filled with concern. "What is going on?"

Lori clumsily pushed past and stepped inside, tears streaming down her face. She lowered herself to the floor and grabbed her knees, folding herself into a small ball. Her skin was mottled, and her hair was unkempt. Meghan had only seen Lori in such a state during the murder scandal several weeks ago, and she felt a lump in her throat as she studied the upset girl in front of her.

"They're dead, Meghan, and it's *our* fault."

Meghan's jaw dropped. "Who? Who is dead, Lori?"

Still huddled on the floor, Lori began to shake. "The Bishops! Brian and Amy? They stopped by our booth last night for brownies, and now, they are *dead!*"

Meghan felt her body grow cold. She tried to maintain composure as she tried to understand what Lori was telling her. After taking a long pause, Meghan shook her head, placing a hand on Lori's shoulder.

"Lori," she said kindly. "Lori, the Bishops' death has nothing to do with us! I baked the brownies myself, and you helped me with everything. It's horrible that they are dead, but I don't think it had *anything* to do with us!"

Lori's somber eyes met Meghan.

"The police are saying it was poison, and they're saying it was from food at the event."

Meghan placed her other hand on Lori's other shoulder.

"Lori," Meghan said, this time with an air of sternness. "Lori, there were dozens of vendors and foods present at the event. There is no way that *my* brownies had anything to do with their deaths. They probably ate pounds of other foods at the event!"

Lori's eyes widened.

"They didn't, Meghan," she whispered. "The police already spoke with their twin sons, Jake and Josh. Jake and Josh went to Fisher Fest with their parents, and they've *sworn* that their parents had dinner out *before* the event. Jake and Josh told the police that their parents have some sort of serious dietary restriction, and they don't usually eat out. Josh said that they made an exception last night with *your* treats, and that he saw *both* of his parents eating them at the event, and that they think *you* had something to do with it!"

Meghan's stomach churned. She felt the lump in her throat grow larger, and tears threatened to cascade down her round cheeks.

"It's our fault, Meghan! They ate our brownies, and now, they are dead!" Lori sobbed.

Meghan lowered herself to the ground and stared into Lori's eyes.

"Do you know *anything* else, Lori?" she asked.

Lori shook her head.

"Everyone in town knows. The Bishop boys found them this morning and went to the police, and now everyone is talking about it! I heard the police will be here soon to interview us. I don't know *how* this happened, Meghan. They've done some testing already, and they're saying that the Bishops' brownies must have been poisoned *during* the event. Oh, Meghan, this is terrible!"

Lori burst into loud, wet, heaving sobs, and Meghan could not contain her emotions any longer. Her brownies and her character were going to be at the center of *another* murder scandal, and as Lori sobbed beside her, Meghan joined in, her own body shaking as fear and sadness consumed her.

Suddenly, there was a loud rap on the door.

"Sandy Bay Police! Open up!"

4

The next few days were a whirlwind, and Meghan felt as though she were living in a nightmare; every single order she had, including the massive corporate order for the Weeks Group, had been unceremoniously canceled despite Meghan *and* Lori's innocence having been declared by the Sandy Bay Police. The police had interviewed both Meghan and Lori on the morning after Fisher Fest, and after a few questions, it was obvious that neither Meghan nor Lori had any knowledge of the Bishops' deaths.

"Both of you should lay low while we sort the rest of this out," Officer Nunan, a seasoned officer, had cautioned the women. "We are confident that neither of you had anything to do with this, but this is a small town, and with Ms. Truman being new around here, and with everything that happened with the murder a few weeks ago, it might be best if you got out of town for a while."

Meghan had stared at Officer Nunan, nodding her head.

"I'll be sending another officer out in a few days to check in and maybe collect a few samples, but like I said, I feel confident that neither of you have anything to do with the deaths," Officer Nunan said, her voice authoritative as she scanned Meghan and Lori's faces. "You both take care now, and if you hear anything, you come straight to me."

Meghan and Lori had nodded obediently at Officer Nunan, and with a tip of her hat, Officer Nunan left the bakery. Almost immediately, the phone began ringing, and Meghan and Lori spent the next three hours taking notes of each and every order cancellation.

"I cannot believe this is happening," Meghan had muttered to herself after her last order was canceled. "Not again."

The chiming of the little silver bells grabbed Meghan's attention, and she looked to the front door of the bakery. Sally Sheridan, one of Sandy Bay's grumpiest older ladies, walked into Truly Sweet, a look of disdain on her wrinkled face.

"Lori," Meghan whispered. "Lori, it's a customer. Put on a nice face!"

Lori wiped the tears from her eyes and pasted a smile on her lips. "Good morning, Mrs. Sheridan!" she chirped.

Mrs. Sheridan vigorously shook her head. "It's *not* a good morning, and I hear this dreadful bakery is to blame once again!"

Meghan bit the inside of her cheek, trying to keep calm.

"Mrs. Sheridan," Meghan replied sweetly. "The police have already been here, and they stated I had nothing to do with the deaths of the Bishops. It's just terrible, but I'm not to blame, and neither is my assistant!"

Mrs. Sheridan frowned. She reached into the large alligator-skin purse draped over her arm and retrieved a small box. Mrs. Sheridan shoved the box to Meghan.

"I want to return this for a full refund!" she declared. "It's one of your brownies from the event last night. These things are poisonous, and I want a refund!"

Meghan cocked her head to the side. "Mrs. Sheridan," she began slowly. "We didn't sell the brownies at Fisher Fest. We simply provided desserts. If you did not purchase the brownie, I cannot give you a refund."

Mrs. Sheridan stared into Meghan's eyes. "That's preposterous! Your brownies *killed* the Bishops, and I *want* a refund!"

Meghan glanced at Lori and could see that her assistant was on the verge of a meltdown. Meghan sighed, but reached into the cash register and pulled out five dollars. She carefully placed each bill on the counter in front of Mrs. Sheridan, and Mrs. Sheridan snatched up the money and hobbled out of the bakery.

"Last time, your apple pie gave me diarrhea, and now, your brownies are killing people! The nerve!" Mrs. Sheridan ranted to herself as she slammed the door behind her.

Meghan could feel her shoulders relax as Mrs. Sheridan left, but Lori did not look relieved.

"Lori," Meghan said gently. "Go home. It's Saturday. Go home, stay home, and don't come back until at least Wednesday. It's going to be quiet here, and you need to take care of yourself."

Lori nodded. She embraced Meghan and left the bakery.

On Tuesday, Meghan was mopping the bakery's wooden floors when she heard a knock at the door. It had been a quiet week; not a single walk-in customer had visited Truly Sweet, and Meghan had started locking the front door as a precaution. People in town had been quite cold; at the grocery on Sunday evening, fellow customers navigated their carts away from Meghan as she walked down the aisles, and the check-out man didn't say a word to her. Meghan could tell that everyone in Sandy Bay thought she was to blame for the Bishops' deaths, and she was worried someone might retaliate against her.

The knocking continued, and Meghan propped the wet mop against the counter and tiptoed to the front door.

"Hello?" Meghan called out.

"Meghan? It's Jack. Jack Irvin?"

Meghan's heart began to flutter. Jack was here to check on her! He had looked so dapper at Fisher Fest, and despite the current situation, Meghan was happy that Jack was here. She threw open the door, and he smiled down at her.

"May I come in?" he asked politely.

Meghan nodded. Seeing the wet floor, Jack edged around the perimeter of the room, stopping to lean against the counter above a dryer patch of floor.

"How are you doing?" Jack asked.

"I'm fine, I guess," Meghan answered. Jack gave her a pitying look.

"Maybe it's time you lay off the brownies for good, Meghan," he answered, gazing up and down her curvy body. Meghan's cheeks grew red. "There is historical proof to show that they do seem to get you in all sorts of trouble."

The fluttering of Meghan's heart stopped; she was irritated by Jack's tone. He was being condescending, and Meghan folded her arms across her chest in response.

"What can I do for you, Officer Irvin?" Meghan asked, adding the formality of Jack's title in her address to let him know that she was displeased.

Jack stepped back, aware that Meghan was annoyed.

"I'm here to check on you. Officer Nunan wanted someone to come out and make sure you are doing alright," he responded.

Meghan nodded her head. "I'm just great," she said. "I'm innocent, but everyone in this town thinks I had something to do with another murder. My orders are all canceled, including the Weeks Group corporate order, and I have no customers."

Jack nodded his head. "Well, sorry to rain more on your parade, but I just wanted to let you know that my team might be coming out later to collect some brownies."

Meghan rolled her eyes. "This is crazy!"

Jack raised one eyebrow. "It's a murder investigation, Meghan," he said. "We have to take every measure to understand what happened."

Meghan narrowed her eyes at Jack. "I saw *you* eating my brownies at the event, *Officer* Irvin," she said. "Who is to say that *you* don't have something to do with this?"

Jack shook his head. "I'm just following procedures, Meghan. Please believe me when I say this isn't personal."

Meghan lowered her head and stared at her feet. "This bakery felt like the one thing I ever did right in my life," she mumbled. "And now, it's all ruined."

Jack shrugged his shoulders. "Well," he said. "Like I said, maybe sweets just aren't for you."

He turned on his heel to leave, and Meghan followed him.

"Thanks for your visit, Officer Irvin," Meghan said curtly as Jack stepped outside.

"No problem," he answered as he walked toward his police car.

Meghan could see Dash, Jack's adorable golden retriever, wagging his tail on the front seat. For an instant, her heart warmed, but as Jack drove away, her heart grew heavy again.

"What am I going to do?" Meghan murmured, going back inside the bakery and locking the door behind her. She returned to her mop, but before she could begin cleaning once more, she heard another knock at the door.

"Go *away*, Officer Irvin!" she yelled, frustrated that Jack had returned.

"Meghan? Meghan! It's me!" Karen Denton shouted. "Come let me in, sweetie!"

Meghan felt relief. Karen was here! She carefully walked to the door and found her dear friend smiling up at her.

"Oh, sweetie!" Karen said, pulling Meghan into her arms. "I'm so sorry about everything that has happened! What a terrible thing! I'm sorry it's taken me so long to get over here to see you; I have been sick with the flu for the last few days, but I'm better now, and I thought my girl might need me!"

Meghan collapsed into Karen's hug, resting her head on Karen's muscular shoulder. Karen stroked Meghan's back as they embraced.

"There, there, love," she whispered to Meghan as Meghan began to cry. "We'll get to the bottom of this!"

"I don't know if I can do this anymore!" Meghan wept into Karen's shoulder. "Opening Truly Sweet made me so happy; I moved here to get a fresh start after my career as an actress in LA didn't take off, and things were going so well. Now, I'm at the center of *another* murder scandal."

"Did I make the biggest mistake of my life by leaving LA and coming to Sandy Bay? Am I really cut out to run a successful bakery business? Oh, Karen! I don't know if I can take this or do this anymore!"

Karen placed a hand under Meghan's chin and guided Meghan's eyes to meet her own. Her eyes were kind, but she spoke with a tone that indicated seriousness.

"Meghan," she began. "You are my dear friend, and like a daughter to me! I adore you, and I refuse to let you be driven out of *my* hometown by this scandal. When I first met you in LA, I knew you were special, and I will not let something like this happen to *my* special friend, or her business! Do you understand me?"

Meghan did not reply, but Karen continued to stare fiercely into her eyes.

"Meghan, when I ran the marathon in Barcelona last summer, my body felt exhausted; I am seventy-two years old, and most women my age don't run like that! Seeing the young people sprint by me left me feeling sorry for myself for almost three whole miles! But you know what? Even though I was tired and down, I didn't give up. Giving up isn't an option! You can't just throw in the towel because of a little trouble. Do you understand me?"

Meghan nodded, thankful for Karen's counsel.

"Good," Karen said. "Meghan, I was born here and raised here, and I know Sandy Bay like the back of my own hand! I know the people here, and I know how things work. I promise you I will do my best to help you figure out what happened to the Bishops and to save Truly Sweet! We'll figure it out, Meghan. Just you wait."

5

The day after karen's visit, the inspiration Meghan had drawn from Karen's pep talk had vanished; it was a dark, rainy morning, and Meghan was curled up in bed with no plans to leave her room. She had only left her bed to slip downstairs into the bakery, fetching a bag of stale, homemade donuts she had found in the pantry. Meghan carried the donuts back upstairs and stuffed each one into her mouth, eventually eating the entire bag.

"At least I have an appetite," Meghan thought to herself as her belly groaned from the mass quantity of sugar she had consumed. "Some people don't eat anything when they are stressed, and at least I will have my strength!"

Meghan snuggled beneath her purple comforter, feeling temporarily safe from the scandal that had sullied her reputation. She rested quietly, and eventually fell into a light slumber, only waking when the telephone began to ring. Meghan had only received one call since Lori's frantic call with news of the Bishops' murder; Kirsty Fisher had called to scream at Meghan, saying that Meghan had ruined her event. Now, as the phone rang, Meghan braced herself.

"Sweetie! Good morning!" Karen greeted. Meghan gave a loud sigh of relief, happy to hear a friendly voice.

"Karen," she said. "How are you?"

Meghan heard Karen giggle. "You sound sleepy, Meghan!"

Meghan looked down at her legs, still wrapped in her blankets. "I'm still in bed."

Karen giggled again. "Well, rise and shine, sweetie! I've already been out for a long run, been to the gym, and gone to yoga this morning!"

Meghan looked down at the empty bag of donuts beside her. "I'm still feeling down, Karen," she admitted.

"Well, you'd best perk up, Meghan! I have some news about the Bishops."

Meghan's eyes grew large, and she gripped the phone tightly. "What's the news?"

"Well, my good friend, Jeanne-Marie, works down at the police station, and I asked her if she knew anything! She said no when I asked last night, but she just phoned me and said that there are several suspects in the Bishop murder case!"

Meghan's heart pounded. "Who are they, Karen?"

"Jeanne-Marie couldn't give me a lot of information, but she did give me the name of two suspects! Jake and Josh Bishop, the adult sons of Brian and Amy Bishop!"

Meghan gasped. "They were at the event! They told the police that I had something to do with the deaths!"

"That sounds too convenient," Karen said. "They just happened to place the blame on *you* and *they* are some of the main suspects? I think we should look into them, Meghan. Get up and get dressed. We have a lot to do today."

"Karen," she said cautiously. "What do you mean?"

"Get up and get dressed, quickly! Put on some dark clothes and tuck your hair back. I have a *fabulous* idea!"

6

"We look ridiculous," Meghan said as Karen guided her orange jeep down the long, winding path leading to the Bishops' house.

Both women were dressed in black from head to toe; Karen wore a black workout jacket, black yoga pants, and a black running hat, while Meghan wore a pair of bedraggled black overalls she had found at the bottom of her wardrobe. Karen had insisted on wearing black ski masks, but Meghan had firmly refused.

"This is what spies wear!" Karen declared, slowing the jeep down as the Bishops' grand house came into view. "When I was a traveling nurse in Moscow, I knew a spy, and this is exactly what she wore when she went on missions!"

Meghan sighed. She was far out of her comfort zone, but Karen's exuberance was contagious, and Meghan *was* hopeful that their bold endeavor could help unearth the truth about the murders.

"We'll park over by the pool house. I called Jamie Cruise, the local handyman? He's done some work around the

Bishop place, and he swore that if I parked by the pool house, no one would see me!"

Meghan looked at Karen incredulously. "How exactly did you explain to Jamie that you and I are going on a spy mission, Karen?"

Karen grinned at Meghan. "I may have agreed to be his spotter at the gym next week; he's always had a little crush on me, and believe it or not, this old lady can still be cute when she wants to be!"

Meghan laughed. "You are too much, Karen Denton," she said, her heart swelling with gratitude for her partner in crime.

They drove by the Bishop house, and Meghan gasped.

"It's enormous," she said breathlessly. "I knew they must have had money if they went to Fisher Fest, but I didn't realize they were this rich!"

Karen nodded. "Wealthy folks, but still very down to Earth. Brian made his fortune selling priceless antiques, and Amy used to be on some show years and years ago. Can't remember the name. Anyway, Brian and Amy are… were… darlings. Such a sweet couple. Their boys, on the other hand, not so much; Josh and Jake are twenty-seven, close to your age, but they are *trouble*! They were in and out of jail as teenagers, but Brian managed to buy them a place at a fancy college abroad. They came back to Sandy Bay refined and handsome after college, but they've done next to nothing since. They nearly ruined Brian and Amy a few years ago; they sank two businesses using money they stole from Amy, and lately, they've just been living in the basement of their parents."

"Ugh," Meghan said. "They sound *awful*! I can't *believe* the town has turned on *me* when the police have already declared me to be innocent! The Bishop twins have already been so bad; why hasn't everyone turned on them?"

Karen shook her head. "Brian and Amy were beloved in this community," she replied. "No one wants to believe that the children of such wonderful people could commit such an act. You are the new girl in town, Meghan. It's easier for these small town Sandy Bay people to blame you."

Karen brought the jeep to a halt and turned to Meghan. "Let's review the plan," she said, her eyes gleaming. "It's nearly ten at night, and from what I've been told, the twins go to bed early. It's dark outside, so even if they *are* awake, no one will see us in our dark outfits! Jamie told me that the basement door is always unlocked, so we will simply walk in!"

Meghan bobbed her head in agreement. "Sounds good," she whispered.

"Then," Karen continued. "We will search the house. Surely if the boys slipped poison to their parents at the event, there will be some evidence! The police didn't search the house, from what I heard, and if they haven't been here yet, there's still a chance we'll find a clue!"

Meghan looked at Karen, her hazel eyes large with concern. "Are you *sure* this is a good idea?" she asked Karen, tugging anxiously at the straps of her overalls as the two women sat in the parked car.

Karen nodded firmly. "Jeanne said that the boys are suspects, and when she and I talked this morning, she told me that the boys have even been overheard saying that they wished their parents were dead so that they could inherit their wealth! Those twins have always been trouble, and with everything they've done to hurt Brian and Amy financially in the last few years, I just think it's a good idea to start with them!"

Karen and Meghan crept out of the car and walked toward the enormous three-story brick house. All the lights were off, but Meghan still felt nervous. Karen led Meghan around to the back, and carefully, Karen jiggled the handle of the back door leading off of the pool area.

"It's open!" Karen whispered in delight. "Follow me!"

Karen and Meghan walked inside. The room was pitch black, and the air was sticky and humid, which was odd, considering it was October in the Pacific Northwest. Karen pulled a flashlight out of the small fanny pack secured around her waist.

"What is this place?" Meghan asked as Karen turned on the light. Karen directed the light around the room, and Meghan could see hundreds of plants lining the walls.

"It's a greenhouse!" Karen exclaimed. "Look at all the plants! I see some tropical things over there. It smells wonderful in here!"

Meghan paused, staring at Karen.

"Karen," she whispered. "Think about it. They have their own greenhouse! What if the twins *grew* whatever poison was used *here*? There are thousands of plants here! Maybe they tucked some little poisonous plant away somewhere!"

Karen pointed the flashlight into Meghan's face. "Maybe you *are* a spy after all, Meghan Truman!"

Before Meghan could reply, the room was suddenly flooded with light.

"What is going on down there?"

The color drained from Meghan's face, and she began to shake. Two tall, handsome men stood peering down at them from the top of a narrow staircase leading down into the greenhouse.

"Mrs. Denton?"

Karen flashed a bright smile at the men.

"Josh! Jake! Hello, boys!"

Josh and Jake Bishop stalked down the stairs. They were identical, both with curly black hair, wire-rimmed glasses, and a smattering of freckles across their cheeks. Meghan had never seen them before, but as they approached her, she saw the resemblance they bore to their father, who Meghan had met at Fisher Fest.

"What are you doing here, Mrs. Denton?"

Both men were staring at Karen. One turned and looked at Meghan, and jerked his chin to gesture at her. "Who is she, Mrs. Denton?"

Karen smiled graciously at the two. "Oh? You haven't met her?" Karen asked. Both men shook their heads.

"Didn't you two know? I volunteered to come care for the plants. The whole town has come together to send up meals for you two, as well as help care for the house. Sandy Bay truly comes together during a tragedy, and I am just doing my part!"

Meghan's jaw dropped, but she quickly forced her own mouth into a smile. She was amazed at how effortlessly Karen had lied to the twins, and she hoped she could be convincing if they questioned her.

"Well, thank you for doing that," said one of the twins. "It's a little late to come over, isn't it?"

Karen tucked a loose hair back into her hat and grinned. "You know me! As a nurse for so many years, my sleep patterns are just silly. I didn't even realize it was so late! We are so sorry to bother you."

Meghan nodded at the door. "We should just be going!"

The other twin moved to stand in front of the door, his eyes fixated on Meghan. "Mrs. Denton," he said, his voice flat. "Who *is* this? Why is she here with you?"

Meghan ordered herself not to flinch, and she bit her bottom lip as she tried to stretch her mouth upwards into a more convincing smile. What was Karen going to say? She had never met the twins before, and if they realized that she was the woman they had blamed for the death of their parents, surely it would not be good.

"This is my granddaughter, Norah!" Karen said with confidence. "She is helping me for the weekend, and I dragged her along to water the plants."

The twin closest to Meghan studied her face, lifting one eyebrow. "Mrs. Denton," he said slowly. "This is a small town, and I know for a fact that you don't have a daughter, which means that this is..."

"My adopted granddaughter! She is the granddaughter of an old friend who died years ago, and this little lady needed a grandma in her life! We've been close for years, and I just adore her."

Meghan fought the urge to clench her fists as the twin stared into her eyes. She batted her eyelashes, hoping that perhaps she could ease the tension.

"Well, we've finished tending to the plants, and it *is* late," Karen said, still smiling at the boys with her blindingly white teeth. "I'll just take Norah and we'll go!"

The twins both nodded. "Yes, it's best if you leave," one said. "We have special care for the plants, so don't worry about coming back," added the other. "So kind of you to come and bring your....granddaughter....but please don't come back."

Karen walked toward the door, and the twins moved out of her way. Meghan quickly followed, and as soon as the door shut behind them, they sprinted back to the jeep. Karen arrived first, barely breaking a sweat, but Meghan panted as she climbed into the passenger seat.

"They're hiding something," Karen said, reapplying a coat of lipstick as Meghan collected herself. "Thank goodness they hadn't met you yet, Meghan! They were acting odd in that greenhouse, and it was clear that they didn't want us there. Imagine if they had known that you were *the* Meghan Truman! It could have gotten ugly."

Meghan wiped a bead of sweat from her brow as she sank back into the passenger seat.

"Let's get out of here," she said to Karen. "I did my best to memorize the leaves and the colors of the unmarked plants. I need to do some research."

Karen turned to Meghan and grinned. "Like I said, you may just be a little spy after all!"

7

"Forget about the twins. I have another suspect," Karen shrieked into the phone. Meghan rolled over to look at her alarm clock.

"Karen?" Meghan said groggily. "It's ten in the morning!"

"It's practically afternoon," Karen replied. "I've been up for an hour at the gym, and Jeanne just called me with some new information! Apparently, Kirsty Fisher's charity, the Fisher Foundation? Meghan, Jeanne told me that it's failing! The Fisher Foundation is sinking *fast* and has been failing for a few months now!"

Meghan turned over and groaned. "What does that have to do with anything?"

Karen sighed into the phone. "Meghan, it's important to know *everything* about the case! This pertains to *you* and *your* business, and I thought you should know! Kirsty Fisher is on the suspect list, and that's something we need to look into!"

"Thank you, Karen," she said. "I'll think about it when I wake up for real later."

"No! Meghan, get up and moving! I'm off to yoga in a few minutes! Why don't you join me? We could go to yoga and then go for a little jog! I've noticed you've been eating a lot of sweets lately, and it might do you some good to----"

Meghan hung up the phone and pulled a pillow over her head. She *had* been indulging lately; with business being non-existent since the death of the Bishops, Meghan had an abundance of ingredients in the kitchen needing to be used. She had baked and consumed several batches of cupcakes, macarons, and éclairs, and she was embarrassed that Karen had noticed.

Later that day, as Meghan sat idly in the bakery, she heard a sharp knock on the door.

"Not again," she groaned, hoping that Jack Irvin had not returned.

"Meghan Truman! Open up the door this instant!" Kirsty Fisher shouted. Meghan's blood turned cold.

"Kirsty," Meghan whispered in disbelief. Had Kirsty somehow found out that Meghan knew about the Fisher Foundation?

Meghan timidly opened the door. Kirsty glared up at her. Her blonde hair tucked into an elegant chignon at the base of her neck, and she was impeccably dressed in a cream suit and matching heels. Small diamonds glittered in her ears, and a little cream hat was tilted atop her head. Despite Kirsty's attire, Meghan noticed that she looked upset; her face was pale, her eyes were red, and her cheeks look gaunt.

"A word," Kirsty hissed, pushing past Meghan and stomping into the bakery. "I brought this back to you; your assistant must have forgotten to pack it up," Kirsty said as she shoved a small flowered plate at Meghan. "Let's talk. I'm *very* unhappy, Meghan. I gave you an opportunity to serve your treats at *my* event, and then the Bishops *died*! I don't care if the police have said you are not to blame; people are *talking*, and who is to say that *you* didn't kill that poor couple? It seems a little odd that you are now at the center of two murder scandals!"

Meghan stared at Kirsty. She tightened her jaw and counted to ten in her head. Meghan wanted to stay collected and cool, but Kirsty continued her rant.

"How *dare* you come in and ruin *my* event with your trashy treats! I did you a favor, and you went and tarnished the Fisher name forever! This is a disgrace, and my foundation is now in shambles because of *you*!"

Meghan's hazel eyes widened, and she counted up to ten and back down to zero, breathing slowly and trying to stay controlled. Kirsty stepped closer to Meghan and stood on her tiptoes, jabbing a manicured finger in Meghan's face.

"I am *disgusted* with this situation," she said, glowering at Meghan. "I shouldn't have even bothered to come around this... this... this kitchen of *death*!"

Meghan's hands clenched into fists, and she saw Kirsty's eyes widen.

"Don't you make fists in front of me!" she screeched, using her sharp nail to poke Meghan's chest.

"Don't touch me," Meghan said, her voice flat, but her eyes ablaze with anger.

"I will touch you if I feel like it! You've gone and ruined *everything*, and I'll do as I please!" Kirsty snapped as she pressed her sharp nail even further into Meghan's collarbone.

Meghan unclenched her fists. She slowly raised her hands and pushed Kirsty away from her.

"How *dare* you?" Kirsty shouted, marching back to Meghan. "Do you know who I am? I should call the police! I took pity on you by taking a chance on your desserts after the murder scandal with Norman Butcher, and I was a *fool* to let some inexperienced, inept buffoon into *my* event!"

"How could you say that to me?" Meghan demanded,

drawing herself up to full height to tower over Kirsty. "That's horrible and unclassy! I didn't even want to do your stupid event, anyway! You pranced in here and more or less forced me to do your event, for free, mind you, and now I am facing the scorn of the town! It's crazy, and you're crazy!"

Meghan shoved Kirsty away again, and Kirsty bumped her bottom against the counter. Kirsty's blue eyes grew large. She stared up at Meghan, and then she burst into tears.

"You are right," she sobbed, leaning forward to wrap her tiny arms around Meghan. Meghan stiffened, unsure of what to do as Kirsty cried in her arms. She awkwardly lifted a hand to pat Kirsty's head, but Kirsty slapped her hand away.

"Don't touch the hair or hat," Kirsty sniffled, still leaning into Meghan. "I'm just so upset! This has been terrible, Meghan!"

Kirsty's vulnerability struck Meghan, and Meghan felt her own eyes fill with tears. She herself then leaned into Kirsty's hug, and the two women embraced.

"I know," Meghan whispered gently. "It's been terrible."

"I'm so sorry," Kirsty said. "I'm just *so* embarrassed. My event was ruined, the Bishops are dead, and I just treated you terribly."

Meghan pulled back to look at her. Kirsty's makeup was still perfectly intact, but she delicately wiped at her eyes with a small handkerchief.

"I must look awful," she whimpered. "Crying is so unattractive!"

Meghan giggled. "It's fine," she said. "You look perfect."

Kirsty let out a soft laugh, and then, both women were consumed with laughter, their stomachs heaving up and down. The long, emotional release was cathartic, and Meghan was thankful to have calmed Kirsty down.

"Look at us!" Kirsty exclaimed. "There's a murderer on the loose, and we're here laughing like children!"

Meghan smiled. "We needed that laugh," she said. "Laughter and brownies can be the best medicine."

Kirsty raised an eyebrow and looked at Meghan's waist. "Looks like you've had a lot of medicine over the last few days," she said. Kirsty then clapped a hand to her mouth. "So sorry," she said. "That was rude."

Still smiling, Meghan placed her hands on her hips and shrugged. "It's fine. We've had a hard week. Don't worry about it. Now, you look like you could use a cup of tea. May I bring you one?"

Kirsty nodded.

Meghan made a cup of black tea and served it to Kirsty in her best glass teapot.

"Perfect!" Kirsty exclaimed. "You have been so sweet. Everyone else has been so aloof this week; it's like they think I planned the murder since it happened at my event! So terrible. If it weren't for my husband, I would be lost right now. He's been taking care of everything. He is such a doll."

Meghan felt her heart sink. Kirsty had looked so sad until she mentioned her husband, and Meghan saw the love and adoration in Kirsty's eyes, just as she had seen it at Fisher Fest.

"You're lucky to have him," Meghan said.

Kirsty nodded. "He's the most wonderful! Do you have anyone special to help you through this terrible time?"

Meghan looked down at the counter and shook her head, wondering if she would ever find someone who could light up her heart as Kirsty's husband did for her. Kirsty's husband had been at Kirsty's side when she was the belle of the ball at Fisher Fest, and it was evident that he was standing by his wife now, even in the darkest of circumstances.

"I don't have anyone," she whispered. "Well, I have Karen Denton, and I have Lori, my assistant. They are great, and I love them to pieces! But a love like yours? I don't know if I'll ever have that, Kirsty."

Kirsty rolled her eyes. "Well, you have enough to worry about!" she declared. "Love is sweet, but so are your treats. I usually don't indulge in any of the delicious sweets you have here, but maybe, just this once….? It can be our little secret."

Meghan laughed. "I'll get a treat for you, Kirsty, no worries. It'll be just between us."

8

"I just don't know what to do, Meghan!" Lori whispered into the phone. "I needed this job. My rent is due soon, and I still have some loans to pay off from school. I can't afford to not work, Meghan. I love working for you at Truly Sweet, but unless business drastically picks up again, I think I'm going to have to find another job."

Meghan groaned. She treasured Lori's company and Lori's help; Lori made an excellent assistant, and she possessed impressive cake decorating skills that Meghan was eager to develop! More importantly, she was loyal and sweet, and Meghan had loved having her around.

"Lori," she said calmly. "Think about this. The police have publicly announced that I'm not responsible for the Bishop murders. Everyone knows that. The people in Sandy Bay just have to come around. They will. You'll see."

Meghan heard Lori breathing loudly. "Lori?" she asked. "Are you alright?"

Lori sniffled. "I think I'm having a panic attack, Meghan! I need money, and I need my job! You aren't from here. People won't just move on unless they have someone new to blame, and the police haven't arrested anyone. Who knows what will happen?"

Meghan held the phone tightly and took a long, deep breath. "Lori," she gently replied. "We'll figure this out. It will be fine. The police have suspects, I know that for a fact!"

Meghan then clapped her hand over her mouth. She had not yet told Lori about her and Karen's own little investigation, and she didn't want to get anyone in trouble.

"What?"

"Lori," she began. "This is secret information. You can't ask questions of me. Let's just say that I know of two main suspects. The police are looking into the twins! They think the twin sons of the Bishops could have done it, and after doing some of my own research, I think there is a good chance they had something to do with it!"

Lori gasped. "That makes sense! Those twins have always been a nuisance in Sandy Bay! They're a few years older than me, and they used to tease me mercilessly at school. They've had some troubles lately; everyone says they stole from Brian Bishop to start their own business, and it would make perfect sense that they orchestrated the murders of their parents! They've always talked about their inheritances, and I wouldn't be surprised if they killed their parents to get their money as soon as they could!"

Meghan thought for a moment. "Lori," she said quietly. "If the twins were trying to get their hands on their money, then that could be proved! Surely the Bishops had a will. But you'd said the twins have been terrible and have taken from their parents already! There's no way that they were the beneficiaries of their parents' will if they've treated them so poorly! There must be another benefactor!"

Lori was quiet, and Meghan imagined she was pondering Meghan's theory.

"Do you know who handles the wills in town, Lori?" she asked.

"Sorry, Meghan, I'm not sure," Lori replied. "When my father died a few weeks ago, he died without a will, and I have no idea."

"No problem, Lori," she said quietly. "Look, give me another week to sort this out. If in a week things haven't changed, I'll write you a check and you can find another job, no hard feelings."

Lori sniffled. "Thanks, Meghan," she said as she hung up.

Meghan immediately called Karen.

"Karen! I need your help!" she exclaimed. "The Bishops' will! If we can get to their will, we can find out if the twins were the beneficiaries of the Bishop estate. If they were, that's a pretty solid motive for killing their parents, and I should tell Jack!"

Karen laughed. "You've been doing some thinking! Fabulous! It sounds like we need to track down that will. Vince Fisher handles all the wills and legal documents in town, and I would bet that he has the answers we need. Get ready; I'm leaving the gym now and will be over to pick you up in five!"

9

Meghan stood nervously in front of the Fishers' front door with Karen. The house, while not as grand as the Bishops', was beautiful, and Meghan felt underdressed in her plain black and white striped tee, jeans, and white sneakers.

"Well! Knock on the door! You said that you and Kirsty shared a little moment, yes? Surely she'll be happy to see you?"

Meghan raised her left hand to her mouth and began to bite her nails.

"Stop that!" Karen said, swatting at Meghan's hand. "Don't you know that billions of germs can get into your body through nail-biting? Now, get your hand out of your mouth and use it to knock on the door!"

Meghan obeyed, and she slowly raised her hand to the large mahogany door. She gave it three quiet taps. No one answered it.

"Well, I guess no one is home!" she said, turning and walking down the steps toward Karen's jeep. "We tried!"

Karen rolled her eyes. "You can be such a chicken sometimes, Meghan Truman!" she declared as she stepped up and began knocking on the door.

"Hello? Hello! Kirsty? Vince? It's me, Karen!"

The door was opened by a blonde-haired woman in a stiff maid's uniform.

"Mrs. Denton! How may I help you?"

"Hello, Cheryl," Karen said warmly. "I just need to speak with Vince and Kirsty for a moment. No emergency, but are they home?"

Cheryl crossed her arms across her chest and shook her head. "They are wrapped up in some things right now and have asked for no visitors," Cheryl answered. "I can tell them you stopped by?"

Karen began to push past Cheryl. "No, Cheryl, we need to speak to them now! It's important!"

"Well, what have we here?"

Meghan heard a man's voice booming in the background. She moved to Karen's side, and from inside the house, she could see Vince Fisher descending a large staircase in the middle of the room.

"Karen Denton! How *are* you?" Vince asked, a smile on his handsome face as he walked to them.

Meghan blushed. Vince was gorgeous, and she could feel her face growing warm as she stared at his angular face and perfectly pressed suit.

Karen smiled at Vince. "I'm well. I just had a little question for you."

"Meghan Truman! Karen Denton! What are you two doing here?"

Meghan saw Kirsty atop the stairs. She was dressed in a violet tea-length dress, and she held what appeared to be a glass of champagne in her hand. Kirsty descended the stairs slowly, her matching violet heels clacking on the marble floors.

"Hi, Kirsty," Meghan said.

"You've caught us at quite the time! I've just learned that the Bishops left their *entire* estate to my charity, the Fisher Foundation! Vince pulled out this bottle of champagne to celebrate! I haven't told many people this, but my charity has been struggling for the last few months, and these unexpected funds will help us survive *and* thrive."

Meghan glanced over at Karen, who was watching Kirsty lean up onto her tiptoes and give Vince a peck on the lips.

"Come in! You *must* celebrate with us."

Karen and Meghan walked into the house together.

"Your house is beautiful, Kirsty," Meghan said, looking at the elegant decor with amazement.

"Oh, how kind of you, Meghan! I'm so happy we've made amends. I had a truly lovely time at Truly Sweet with you."

"Mrs. Fisher?" Everyone turned to Cheryl, who walked into the room holding a cordless telephone. "Officer Irvin is on the phone; he is asking to speak with you."

Meghan felt her heart drop at the mention of Jack's name.

"I have *guests,* Cheryl. What does he want?" Kirsty asked, her voice filled with annoyance.

"He says he has some things to follow up about concerning the Bishop investigation. He says he has some confidential information to discuss with Mr. Fisher."

Kirsty rolled her eyes. "Just tell him we're busy and I will call him back later," she said, folding her hands neatly in front of her.

Cheryl shook her head. "He says it's urgent, Mrs. Fisher. He says he is going to stop over."

Kirsty sighed. "Fine," she replied. "Just have him chat with Vince first; I'm going to visit with my guests, and Officer Irvin will have to wait his turn!"

Cheryl nodded and left the room. Kirsty crossed her arms

in front of her chest, the pearl necklace on her bosom jingling as it moved.

"Admittedly, I was surprised that the Bishops left us their money; Amy and I have never been quite close, but they were loyal patrons of the Fisher Foundation, and with those terrible sons of theirs...well, it isn't a wonder that they didn't let their wealth go to waste! I can use this money for several little projects in town, and their legacy will live on forever."

Vince smiled at his wife. "I have some things to attend to before Officer Irvin gets here. Do you mind if I excuse myself, dear?"

Kirsty nodded. "Of course! I'll take Meghan and Karen to my office to visit."

Karen shook her head. "I forgot my water bottle and midday meal in the jeep; I'm training for another marathon and need to stay hydrated and fed. You two go chat; I'm going to go grab my things. Be right with you."

Kirsty smiled. "Of course, you go. Meghan and I can visit."

Kirsty wrapped her small hand around Meghan's wrist and pulled Meghan down a long hallway.

"My office is this way. It was designed to look just like Kate Middleton's private office at Buckingham Palace. You *do* know who Kate Middleton is, right?"

Kirsty dragged Meghan into a large, airy room. Light shone in from six floor-to-ceiling windows, and there were vases of crisp, white roses everywhere. Kirsty gestured at an overstuffed white satin chair. Meghan sat down, and while she leaned back into the chair, her eyes scanned the room for clues.

"My, my, my... silly me," Kirsty murmured after settling into her own chair. "I forgot refreshments! What a poor host I am. I'll go call for Cheryl, and she can bring some refreshments." Kirsty bustled away, her high heels clacking.

A large glass desk stood in the middle of Kirsty's office. It matched the decor perfectly, but from her position in the chair, Meghan could see one drawer that was not made of glass. It was dark and unsightly, and amidst the splendor of Kirsty's office, it did not match the decor.

"That's strange," Meghan thought to herself. "Why would Mrs. Matchy-Matchy have one ugly desk drawer?"

Meghan rose from her chair and began rummaging through the glass drawers of Kirsty's desk. It was brimming with files and documents, but everything was for Kirsty's sorority alumnae chapter, medical files, and the deeds to the Fishers' three houses.

"I wonder what she's put into the ugly drawer?" Meghan thought aloud as she tried to slide it open. The drawer was locked, but Meghan pulled a bobby pin from her hair and jammed open the lock. She pulled out a single black folder. It was thick, and as she opened it, papers fell out and onto the floor.

"Oh no," Meghan whispered, hoping that Kirsty would not find her with paperwork on the floor. "What are these?"

Meghan read the first piece of paper she retrieved from the floor. It was a bill from a casino in Monaco for over three hundred fifty-thousand dollars!

"What on Earth," Meghan muttered as she looked at the next piece of paper, a receipt for a hotel in Colombia. The receipt was in Vince's name, and Meghan continued rummaging through the papers. Each paper was a bill or receipt for an extravagant hotel and casino. Meghan did not understand. The Fishers were well off, but they weren't wealthy; Karen had told Meghan that most of Kirsty and Vince's money was tied up in a fancy nursing home for Kirsty's ailing mother, and that while the couple presented themselves well, they were not as prosperous as they had been in years past. How were the Fishers affording such magnificent excursions if their money was an issue? Meghan wrinkled her nose in confusion.

Suddenly, Meghan was struck with clarity. She glanced down at the bottom of each piece of paper and found the same signature: THE FISHER FOUNDATION. She gasped. The Fishers had been taking money from their own charity to pay for these elaborate trips, and Meghan had proof! What if the Fishers had also used Vince's role as the most prestigious attorney in town to somehow cheat the Bishops of their wealth? What if the Fishers had arranged for the *murder*? Meghan hastily gathered the paperwork back into the file; she could sneak out with the information and turn it over to the police.

"I know what you two did," Meghan said to herself, furrowing her brow as she stuffed paperwork back into the file folder.

"Oh, *do you?*"

Meghan looked up. Vince Fisher was standing in the doorway, a hand on his hip and a sneer on his face.

10

"What on earth are you doing going through my wife's office?" Vince demanded as Meghan's hazel eyes widened.

"I… I…," Meghan stammered.

Seeing the concerned look on Meghan's face, Vince softened. "I'm sure you didn't mean to snoop," he said carefully. "I'm sure it was just an accident. Why don't you put that folder back right now and let's have a little chat?"

Meghan's hands were shaking, and she placed the folder back into its place.

"Good girl," he said. "Come, sit down."

Meghan stared at Vince, and he smiled back at her.

"I don't know what you think you saw in that file," he began. "But those are *private* documents. Let's just forget all about this and go have a glass of champagne with my wife! She's very excited that the Bishops left their money to our foundation, and I'm sure you would like to wish her well."

Meghan narrowed her eyes at Vince and folded her arms across her chest. "I don't really understand why the foundation is paying for such fancy trips when as of yesterday, it was nearly in financial ruin," Meghan said, gesturing at the drawer where she had returned the file. "It's pretty convenient that the two of you stumbled into this money at just the right time, isn't it?"

Vince rose to his feet and stood directly in front of Meghan. He smiled, but the smile was menacing; Meghan could see the disdain in his eyes, and his pupils grew small as he peered down at her.

"So it's going to be this way, huh? Don't say I didn't give you a chance to pretend like I didn't find you snooping," he said. "You're smart enough. You saw the files. You know what happened."

Meghan glared up at Vince. "You fixed their will to leave their money to the foundation to cover up for you and your wife!"

Vince shook his head. "Have you *met* Kirsty? She had nothing to do with this. I started gambling a few years back. Things turned sour. I handle the finances for the foundation, and it was easy to shift some money here, there, and everywhere I needed it."

Meghan glowered. "You reworked the will and stole their money to cover up for your mistakes. You killed the Bishops at your own event!"

Vince shook his head. "Meghan," he said. "I had to do what I had to do. I didn't want to kill them; Brian and Amy have always been a nice couple. But, sometimes, when you're desperate, you have to do things you don't want to. They were my best chance to restore the foundation, and it worked!"

Meghan rose to her feet. She was standing nose-to-be with Vince, and she could feel his hot breath on her face.

"Sit down," he growled. "You will not ruin this. I've done too much. I'll be disbarred. I'll lose my business."

"I've already lost my business because of you!" she yelled.

She lunged, grabbing for Vince's neck. Vince ducked out of her way, and Meghan crashed into the glass desk in the center of the room.

"You stupid girl!" he snarled. "I gave you a chance to walk away from this, but you've made your choice. I'll end you like I ended the Bishops!"

Vince ran toward Meghan, his fists in front of his face. He reeled back his left fist and pushed it into Meghan's head.

"Stop!" Meghan screamed. She leaned over and kicked, but she did not manage to strike him. Vince wrapped his hands around her neck.

"That'll be the end of you," he said.

He squeezed Meghan's neck tightly, and she struggled to breathe. Slowly, his grip tightened, and Meghan began to see black spots. She could feel her heart beating furiously in her chest, and her body was hot. Vince's fingernails dug into her neck, and she could feel the skin breaking.

"Goodbye," Vince whispered as he squeezed even tighter.

The black spots in Meghan's vision grew, and soon, she was consumed in the darkness. Her consciousness was slipping away, and the memories of her time in Sandy Bay flashed before her eyes. She thought of how much she adored her friendship with Lori, how kind Karen had been to her, and how she would never realize her dream of turning Truly Sweet into a wild success. Meghan let out a soft moan; this was *not* the ending she had expected...

11

"What is going on here?" Meghan heard Kirsty wail.

There was a loud crash, and just as Meghan began to drift into unconsciousness, Vince's grip on her neck immediately loosened. He clumsily tumbled on top of her.

"Officer Irvin! What are you *doing*?" Kirsty screamed.

Meghan blinked open her eyes and saw Jack Irvin standing over Vince with the handle of a teapot in his hands. The body of the teapot lay in pieces on the floor, and it was clear that Jack had broken it over Vince's head.

"Get off of my husband! Explain yourself!" she screeched at Jack. Vince rubbed his head; there was blood pouring from a large gash on his forehead, and he moaned.

"Meghan!" Jack cried out. "You!" he yelled down at Vince. He quickly removed a pair of handcuffs from his belt and secured Vince's arms.

"What is happening?" Kirsty sobbed as Jack restrained her husband. "Officer Irvin? Why is my husband in handcuffs? What is going on here?"

Jack shook his head. "Ma'am," he began solemnly. "We've

had our eye on Mr. Fisher for the last few months; we've been monitoring Vince's accounts, along with the accounts of your foundation, and things were not adding up. There's been an odd trail of money in and out to several casinos around the world, and from what we've pieced together, Mr. Fisher is at the center of one of the biggest scandals of money laundering, illegal casinos, and embezzlement in the history of the Pacific Northwest."

"That's impossible!" Kirsty declared. "We are pillars of this community! We have been *servants* to the people and charities of Sandy Bay for *years*! This is a mistake!"

Jack shook his head. "From our records, it's clear that Mr. Fisher has had a gambling issue for several years. We found that he has been siphoning money out of the Fisher Foundation accounts, Mrs. Fisher."

Kirsty's eyes grew wide. "He… took from *our* charity?"

Jack nodded.

"My charity has been in the red," she whispered, her voice quivering. "Vince said the money ran out because *I* made a mistake with the accounts. He said it was my fault. I was so relieved to get the money from the Bishops because it put the Fisher Foundation back on top…"

Jack shook his head. "No, Mrs. Fisher. From what the investigators learned, Mr. Fisher is responsible for a considerable sum of the Foundation's money disappearing, not you."

Kirsty glared at her husband. "Vince. Is this true?" Vince said nothing, and tears began to stream down Kirsty's cheeks. She threw a hand to her forehead and fainted, her small body hitting the floor with a loud thump.

"What is going on in here?" Karen yelled as she bustled into the room. "I went out for fifteen minutes to eat my snack, and I come back to this? What is going on?"

Jack glared down at Vince. "Mr. Fisher here has a lot of explaining to do to his wife and the authorities," he said.

"And the Bishop twins," Meghan mumbled. Jack turned to stare at her.

"What did you say?" Jack asked.

Meghan nodded. "He told me everything. He killed the Bishops and rearranged their will to exclude their sons. He was going to use the money from their estate to cover his tracks with the Fisher Foundation."

Karen's eyes glimmered. "That's my girl," she whispered.

Jack nodded at Karen. "Can you check on her?" Jack asked, gesturing at Kirsty. "You were a nurse, and she fainted."

Karen checked Kirsty's pulse and gently shook her. "Come on, Kirsty," she cooed. "Let's get up, girl!"

Kirsty's eyes slowly opened, and as she saw her husband in handcuffs, she narrowed her eyes.

"This explains everything!" Kirsty shouted. "This explains why you were *always* gone away on business. I thought you were having an affair! All of this time, you were traveling to casinos overseas to gamble, and you used *our* foundation money to do it? You are horrible, Vince. I am disgusted! I am ashamed!" Kirsty dramatically raised a hand to her forehead and slumped against the couch. "How will I ever recover from this filth?"

Jack looked sadly at Kirsty. "I'm sorry, ma'am," he said. "We will need to seize your documents, as well as your husband. I will, however, promise you that your name is now officially cleared; you are no longer a suspect in the murder case."

Kirsty glared. "Well, that just solves everything, doesn't it? I am *ruined*! Vince, I will never speak to you again! I'm calling a lawyer *tomorrow*, and you will have nothing left after I am through with you!"

Jack whispered into his radio, and suddenly, ten police officers burst into the room, led by Officer Nunan.

"Good work, son," she said to Jack.

Jack shook his head. "Meghan figured it out. She put the pieces together."

Officer Nunan turned to Meghan. "Well, then! Outstanding work, Ms. Truman. Well done."

Meghan smiled weakly; her neck hurt from Vince's hands, and she was bleeding from where his nails cut her skin.

"Officer Irvin, radio an ambulance," Officer Nunan ordered. "Let's get this criminal out of here and let's get this hero checked out."

The ambulance arrived, and as Meghan was loaded into the back, Jack walked alongside her gurney.

"You really showed us what you're made of," Jack said in admiration. He reached over and gently touched her hand. "Get well soon, Meghan," he said. "You're a hero today, that's for sure!"

Meghan closed her eyes, happy to be safe, and happy that the killer had been found.

"Yeah," she replied to Jack as she was lifted into the ambulance. "I really was."

As the ambulance sped through the streets of Sandy Bay, Meghan cast her mind back to the image of Kirsty and Vince on the evening of Fisher Fest. They looked so professional, so beautiful, so in love. She couldn't believe that behind that façade was a marriage that had an underbelly that stunk of lies and deception. As she gazed at them that evening, she really wanted what they had. She imagined that there were other people in the room that day that shared her exact thoughts. Only by virtue of her personal interaction with Vince did she realize that not all that glitters is gold.

12

Two weeks after the encounter with Vince, Meghan had returned to work at Truly Sweet. Thanks to a glowing article about her bravery in the face of the killer, business was booming once again, and Lori had also returned to work.

"It's nice to be back," Lori said cheerfully as she tied her apron on for the first time in nearly a month. "I'm ready for things to be *quiet* around Sandy Bay!"

Meghan nodded. Her first months in Sandy Bay had been anything but quiet, and Meghan ached for a sense of normalcy. She secured her own apron and stepped up to the counter.

"I just can't *believe* how he poisoned them," Lori said. "It's terrible! Who would have expected Vince Fisher would have poisoned the Bishops with a little piece of peppermint gum?"

Meghan shrugged her shoulders. "It's crazy," she said. "I heard a witness came forward after Vince was apprehended and said he saw Vince slip Mr. Bishop some gum in the men's restroom right before the event ended! The police tested the gum during the autopsy, and they determined it was poisoned. Thank goodness no one else tried it."

Lori looked down at the counter, her eyes filling with tears. "Amy tried it," she said.

Meghan turned to hug Lori. "It's okay now," she said. "The killer has been caught. Business is good again! The Weeks Group even restored their original order! It's all going to be fine, Lori."

Lori nodded, and the pair got to work. Just as Meghan finished the final touches on a black forest cake, she heard the chime of the little silver bells on the front door. Jack Irvin, dressed in street clothes, walked through the door with Dash, his dog.

"Meghan," he said kindly. "Mind if we chat a minute?"

Meghan felt her cheeks grow warm, and she bobbed her head up and down. "Let me get something for you," she said. Jack sat down at a table, and Meghan joined him a moment later with a large slice of the black forest cake.

"For me?" he asked.

"It's the least I could do," she said. "You gave so much information to the reporters, and thanks to their article, everyone knows that my cooking had nothing to do with the death of the Bishops! You said so many nice things. Thank you."

Jack smiled weakly. "It was the least *I* could do," he said. "The police department knew your desserts had nothing to do with the murders, but since the rumor was going around, we had to let it fly. We hoped the killer would eventually let his guard down since everyone in Sandy Bay seemed to blame you. I'm so sorry, Meghan."

Meghan shrugged. "Everything is fine. Let's just forget about this mess. Go ahead, enjoy your cake. I even brought something for Dash."

Meghan placed a dog-shaped cookie in front of the dog, and Dash tore into it, pieces flying everywhere.

"I'm glad to see that someone likes my treats!" Meghan said, laughing as Dash inhaled the treat. "He's so sweet. It makes me think of getting my own dog."

Jack grinned. "I know a lot about dogs," he said. "Maybe we could talk about them sometime? I could help you when you're making the decision about which one to buy?"

Meghan beamed. She was blushing, but she didn't care. She lowered her eyes and then glanced back up at Jack. He was still smiling at her.

"That would be great, Jack," she said.

"Wonderful! It's a date!" he said.

"It's a date," Meghan replied.

The End

AFTERWORD

Thank you for reading Brownies and Dark Shadows. I really hope you enjoyed reading it as much as I had writing it!

If you have a minute, please consider leaving a review on Amazon, GoodReads and/or Bookbub.

Many thanks in advance for your support!

COOKIES AND BURIED SECRETS

CHAPTER 1 SNEEK PEEK

ABOUT COOKIES AND BURIED SECRETS

Released: August, 2018
Series: Book 3 – Sandy Bay Cozy Mystery Series
Standalone: Yes
Cliff-hanger: No

When a beautiful stranger sashays into a birthday party, Meghan Truman, along with other guests, is surprised to discover her relationship to the birthday celebrant.

This beautiful stranger attracts more shady characters to Sandy Bay. When one of these characters is found dead in an alley, the whole town is set on edge.

Will Meghan's attempt to link the owner of a golden antique gun to the murder prove helpful to handsome Officer Irvin's investigation or will the discovery of a buried secret lead to more murders?

CHAPTER 1 SNEEK PEEK

It was a brisk morning, and Meghan Truman pulled the collar of her blue coat to cover her exposed neck as the chilly breeze nipped at her bare skin. She shivered as the salty air flew off of the ocean and ruffled her dark hair, but she did not move from her spot on the beach. Meghan had moved from Los Angeles to Sandy Bay a few months ago, and while she wasn't quite used to the cool weather and dark skies of the Pacific Northwest yet, she was enjoying the change of pace.

"Hey! Meghan!"

Meghan's heart fluttered as she heard the deep, familiar voice of Jack Irvin. She took a long, deep breath, trying to contain her excitement before turning around to greet him.

"Meghan!"

Meghan slowly pivoted to look up into Jack's handsome face. She grinned, her dark eyes dancing as Jack smiled down at her, his blue eyes sparkling.

"It's good running into you. What are you up to? All alone at the beach, huh?" Jack asked.

"I don't mind," she said, tucking a lock of dark hair

behind her ear. "It's so beautiful here. The beaches in LA were always so crowded, and I love having some peace and quiet."

Jack chuckled. "I wouldn't say you've had a lot of peace and quiet since you've been here," he said, and Meghan lowered her eyes, shifting uncomfortably as she stood in the white sand. "You opened your bakery and then Norman Butcher was murdered, and then that couple was murdered, and you just seem to find your way into the middle of it all."

Meghan's jaw dropped. She was shocked by Jack's words, and her dark eyes filled with tears as she recalled the murders that had scandalized Sandy Bay and almost ruined Meghan's bakery, Truly Sweet.

"Hey," Jack said as he saw the look on Meghan's face. "I didn't mean to say it like that. I'm sorry. The murders in town weren't your fault, and it wasn't your fault that your name got tied up in both situations. I shouldn't have said that."

Meghan turned away from Jack to face the sea, struggling to keep the tears from spilling onto her pale cheeks. She and Jack had *finally* started getting along; Meghan had even developed some romantic feelings for him, but his joke was simply uncouth.

"Meghan," he said, reaching out to gently touch her shoulder. "I'm sorry. Let me make it up to you. I'll be at Karen Denton's birthday party tonight. It's going to be a fun time. Let me pick you up for a nice dinner beforehand."

Meghan blushed. She and Jack had been out together a few times, but nothing had ever come out of their few dinner dates. Was this the chance for something to happen between her and Jack?

"Okay," she said, turning back to look at Jack. "Dinner, and then Karen's birthday party."

"Great!" he said, turning to leave the beach. "I'll see you tonight. It'll be something, I promise."

That night, Jack picked Meghan up in his squad car and took her to dinner at *Feast*, a farm-to-table restaurant in Sandy Bay. Meghan had worn her favorite dress, a form-fitting green dress that accentuated her curves and brought out her dark eyes, and she felt confident as she sashayed to Jack's car.

"You look great!" Jack had said as Meghan answered the door. "Let's have a good night."

After dinner, they drove to Winston's Bar, a local watering hole. Jack escorted Meghan inside, and she saw that Karen's birthday party was well underway. Streamers had been hung from the rafters of the bar, and a band was playing in the corner. Jack led Meghan to a stool at the bar and helped Meghan climb onto it.

"Here you go, ma'am," he said, pushing his blond hair back from his face as Meghan settled in. "I'll go get us some snacks."

"Perfect," she cooed. "I made all the food here myself; I hope you like what Karen requested."

Jack returned five minutes later with two cookies in hand. He handed one to Meghan and then took a large bite out of his. Meghan watched as his eyes widened, and he swallowed the cookie as quickly as he could.

"You know I *love* your treats," he whispered to Meghan, their heads huddled close together. "These spinach-almond-quinoa cookies just aren't hitting the spot for me. Did you bring any of your brownies? Your brownies are out of this world."

Meghan's eyes sparkled at the compliment, and she nodded at Jack. "Ssshhh, let's watch Karen blow out her candles, and then I'll go get some of the brownies I brought. I left a whole pan in the back."

Jack grinned, and he gestured at Karen Denton, Meghan's dear friend. "With her insistence on healthy cookies, not to mention the size of her biceps, you would think she's turning twenty-three, not seventy-three."

Meghan laughed. "Hey, if these spinach-almond-quinoa cookies are the secret to having that much vigor and energy in my seventies, I'll take them over my brownies *any* day."

Meghan edged off of the stool and made her way into Winston's kitchen. As she scanned the room for her pan of brownies, she felt a strong tug on her arm.

"Meghan! Sweetie, hello. I saw you walk in with Jack Irvin. How fabulous. I want to hear *all* the details."

Meghan grinned as the birthday girl, Karen Denton, peered up at her, her blue eyes glittering. "We had dinner before your party," she whispered to Karen, pulling her deeper into the kitchen. "It was *his* suggestion."

"Fabulous!" Karen squealed. "I could not ask for a better birthday present. I've always liked that Jack Irvin, and you know I just think the world of you. I'll keep my fingers crossed. Maybe by my next birthday, you two will be a real couple."

Meghan giggled. "We'll see," she said, reaching to hug Karen. "Enough about me. How are you enjoying your party?"

Karen beamed. "It's exactly what I wanted. I don't have a family of my own, but everyone in Sandy Bay came together to celebrate my birthday. It's just *fabulous*. Everyone is here, Winston kindly opened his bar for us, and those healthy cookies you baked for me are a delight. This old lady couldn't ask for *anything* more on her birthday."

After finishing their hug, the two women turned to walk back into the main area of Winston's bar. Meghan had a plate of brownies for Jack, and she could feel her body growing warm as she caught his eye from across the room. Jack looked so handsome in his blue button-down shirt, and Meghan turned to gush to Karen about how happy she was to be at the party with him. Before she could whisper into Karen's ear, however, Karen stopped in the middle of the room.

"Oh my," Karen stammered, her blue eyes large. A stunningly beautiful woman was walking toward them; she had waist-length black hair, enormous brown eyes, and tan skin. A flower tattoo snaked around her right bicep, and Meghan cocked her head to the side as the woman approached.

"Are you alright?" Meghan asked, looking at Karen with concern. "Who is that?"

Karen's mouth opened, and she clasped a hand to her chest.

"It's my… my… my... it's my *daughter*."

* * *

You can order your copy of **Cookies and Buried Secrets** at any good online retailer.

A SANDY BAY 3 COZY MYSTERY

Cookies and Buried Secrets

AMBER CREWES

ALSO BY AMBER CREWES
THE SANDY BAY COZY MYSTERY SERIES

Apple Pie and Trouble
Brownies and Dark Shadows
Cookies and Buried Secrets
Donuts and Disaster
Éclairs and Lethal Layers
Finger Foods and Missing Legs
Gingerbread and Scary Endings
Hot Chocolate and Cold Bodies
Ice Cream and Guilty Pleasures
Jingle Bells and Deadly Smells
King Cake and Grave Mistakes
Lemon Tarts and Fiery Darts
Muffins and Coffins
Nuts and a Choking Corpse
Orange Mousse and a Fatal Truce
Peaches and Crime
Queen Tarts and a Christmas Nightmare
Rhubarb Pie and Revenge
Slaughter of the Wedding Cake
Tiramisu and Terror
Urchin Dishes and Deadly Wishes
Velvet Cake and Murder
Whoopie Pies and Deadly Lies
Xylose Treats and Killer Sweets

NEWSLETTER SIGNUP

Want **FREE** COPIES OF FUTURE **AMBER CREWES** BOOKS, FIRST NOTIFICATION OF NEW RELEASES, CONTESTS AND GIVEAWAYS?

GO TO THE LINK BELOW TO SIGN UP TO THE NEWSLETTER!

www.AmberCrewes.com/cozylist

Printed in Great Britain
by Amazon